Pencil & Paper

Mission: To Proclaim Transformation and Truth
Publisher: Transformed Publishing, Cocoa, FL
Website: www.transformedpublishing.com
Email: transformedpublishing@gmail.com

ISBN: 978-1-953241-87-0 (paperback)

Pencil & Paper

Melina Trine

Dedication

To my mentors, family, and friends,
I would never have been brave enough
to dream this far without you.

Thank you for your never-ending support
and for the opportunity to make you proud.

Table of Contents

Prologue

Electronic inventions emerged in the 1800's. New awe-inspiring creations birthed by human hands. This initiative single-handedly changed the future, making every-day tasks more efficient, introducing new ways of fun, and assisting humankind in aspects other tools simply couldn't. After all, electronics exist: to help others, to let people not only thrive but to grow, and to give them the ability to chase dreams they once thought wouldn't be possible. Yet, as technology continued to blossom under artificial lights, its purpose distorted.

The most commonly used devices, inadvertently progressed from helpful assistance to machines used for distraction. What was once meant to help people innovate was slowly mutating into something holding us back. The intention of electronics morphed; it grew greedy, when it was supposed to help people do their jobs more efficiently, it wanted the power for itself. Devices began to steal, thieving artists' work and others' ideas, trying to replicate them as their own. But nothing can compare to the passion of humankind, and nothing can truly recreate it. All *it* could manage was to repeat the same vision, over and over. Still, the ease of electronics, increasingly utilized for longer periods of time throughout the day, incorporated into more and more tasks, over the years, eventually became the only thing people used to create; Artificial Intelligence (AI) grew like a weed, while imagination wilted and died. Those who struggled against it, who tried to pluck the weed from the soil, soon found its roots had dug too deep to tear up.

AI was no longer a luxury item, but a requirement, a need, just like the air in someone's lungs. Being utilized helplessly by those who no longer knew how to think without an overproduced answer spat at their feet. It crushed the dreams of everyone in its way, until humans forgot what being creative even meant.

By 2050, electronics had taken over. It didn't happen in the way most popular movies predicted. There was no great war, no big struggle or worldwide apocalypse, just an invention slowly corrupted into a beast, like a once loyal pet that destroyed their own master. Just two hundred fifteen years since the creation of technology, humanity was overthrown. Humans, an animal with the biggest potential, demolished by their own product.

By 2100, no one could tear their eyes away from a screen and no one wanted to. The thought itself was absurd; the idea that anything could be better than the miniature computer they held worshipfully in their palms was unheard of. No one thought for themselves, no one socialized, no one worked or had hobbies; people became husks of what had once been potential. Bodies wandering without purpose, minds constantly stimulated but with no true knowledge to hang on to.

AI eventually came to a standstill; no one was inventing new things, and technology cannot run on its own. With no master to control it, the beast repeats only what it knows, but can never understand anything more. People are too dazed to notice, too lost in their own trances to realize everything is in a never-ending loop.

Yet, there's still hope.

There's always going to be hope.

We simply have to make the wheel stop turning, to halt the loop in its tracks. What'll happen when someone breaks free? Alora's about to find out.

1

Boredom The subway tram was quiet, the type of silence that buzzes in Alora's ears louder than if she had her headphones blasting at top volume. And even though the car is packed with people, crammed in side by side, shoulder to shoulder, like matches in a matchbox, no words are shared. No one is talking, no one breaks the hush. *Why would they?* There's no need to make noise or for senseless conversation when their eyes can stay easily trained on their smart devices, fingers mindlessly swiping, scrolling, and typing. Their faces remain bland, mouths drawn into thin lines, and their eyes watery from the man-made light.

Alora wishes she were them, listening to her own music, or watching the new videos on her feed, or checking to see if her favorite robot influencers posted something new.

Unfortunately for Alora, she lost her E-Device in her rush to get back home. She had feared, at the time, that if she wasn't quick enough, she would miss her subway tram. The next one wouldn't arrive until five minutes later, which, in Alora's world, is an incredibly long time. When everything moves so quickly with just the touch of a button, or a word on a keyboard, a few seconds is long enough for anyone to lose their focus.

In Alora's hurry, her E-Device fell from her jacket pocket, floating to the floor and landing as softly as a newborn being put in its crib, a new update made to stop it from breaking. Alora didn't notice it was missing until she had taken her seat on the tram and reached into her pocket, searching for the familiar, comforting weight of it, only for her fingers to be met with nothing. Now, here she is, with nothing to do, nothing to look at, to scroll through, to listen to, and certainly nothing to keep her from becoming absolutely, and terribly bored.

The feeling is like an itch beneath her skin, and it makes something nasty churn in her stomach. It was as if every second that passed her by only made her more and more queasy, with a sense of doom creeping up the back of her neck like an invisible spider. It was worse than her normal anxiety, the one she usually feels when she forgets her E-Device in another room, or when the low battery warning flashes onto the screen. This feeling is annoying. It refuses to leave her alone, like as if there was something in her sock poking her, she can't find; or the tag of a shirt scraping against her back. It makes her uncomfortable and squirmy.

Poor Alora hasn't felt this feeling before. She has never gone more than a minute without having something to do, to distract her, to put her mind at ease, and make the seconds tick by faster. In fact, she even considered she might be getting sick, even though she had been feeling fine just this morning. It wasn't until she sat down on the tram that the feeling, the one she didn't know the name for, took hold of her.

But Alora longed for a distraction, something to keep her mind off her sudden new emotion. So, she looks at the person seated beside her, a very short, elderly man, who was slumped over an older model electronic, which is practically a dinosaur compared to the new E-Devices. She bends her neck until it aches, leaning in, looking from different angles, and the man never takes notice. Alora isn't even sure the man can see her, despite being sat so close she could feel his breath on her shoulder. Still, no matter how hard she tries, the protective screen recognition prevents her from seeing what holds the man's attention so steadily. She isn't any luckier looking at the device of the girl on her other side or squinting at the woman standing in front of her, whose hand is slowly slipping from the handlebar in her distraction.

Frustrated, Alora sighs and slumps back against her chair, sliding a few inches into the seat, which she's realizing for the first time isn't all that comfortable. Even worse, the feeling in her is growing stronger, hungry for something to do, anything at all.

Alora swiftly looks around, her brown eyes darting from the bland, smooth floor to the slightly tinted windows, which only give her a view of the underground tunnel she's traveling through. She even glances up at the old, surprisingly outdated advertisements near the roof of the tram, with their fading LED lights that keep flickering in and out. Yet, no matter what she tries, nothing seems to be enough, nothing feeds the feeling inside her, and her boredom only grows.

She's about to admit defeat, to settle into the gloom of the feeling, the dullness it promises, and the complete sickening blandness of having nothing to do when she suddenly hears a sound from the other side of the tram. It's loud in the usual silence, echoing off the metal walls around Alora and straight into her ears like the song of an angel. It's just a short, sudden bark of laughter, over as quickly as it began, but it nearly made the poor girl jump from her seat like a startled cat.

No one else in the entire car reacts to the noise, their earbuds engulfed them completely in whatever they are already listening to. The people remain unchanged, still staring at the screen in their hands, their fingers never faltering as they swipe, click, or type; each person's fingers nearly move in unison. It was as if they couldn't be bothered to notice, not as long as they held their own little worlds in their palms. But to Alora, it was something new, something interesting that gave pause to the threat of a never-ending, uninteresting life with no E-Device.

Instantly, Alora straightens in her seat, like a dog that's caught the scent of its favorite human. She's never actually heard someone else laugh before, never paid attention to anything other than her own giggles. This person's laugh was quite different from her own, yet just as bright and filled with joy. Alora peered down the large, long space between her and whoever made the sound. Her eyes wide, searching for a sign, like a smile, or raised eyebrows, or really any small change in one of the passengers' faces. But the car is too long for her to see all the way down, and the people who she does see look no different than they did when the ride first started.

Alora fears she must look like she's crazy, leaning halfway out of her seat, gripping the edges of her chair to make sure she doesn't fall forward, just to try to find one new thing to look at. Still, as she settles once more into her seat, she can't help but wonder, *who laughed and why?* Maybe they watched a funny video, or their AI chatbot told them a joke, or someone in a movie did something stupid, or maybe they even came across an avatar in a game with a ridiculous design.

The thoughts flood Alora's brain, the second she questions the laughter, storming her mind so fast, it feels almost unnatural. It's like a dam has suddenly broken, and the whole sea is pouring through the gaps. And they don't stop; new questions keep popping up like wildflowers blooming in the spring: *If it were a video, was it a short one or a long one? Is it maybe a show I've seen? If it's so funny, should I watch it, or would I not under-stand the joke? In fact, what type of joke would it be? What did this particular stranger find funny?*

Alora was never bombarded with so many questions in her whole life; in fact, she's not even sure she's had so many thoughts at the same time. Usually, with her E-Device, every-thing flashes by so quickly she never has a chance to question it, much less a reason to. If you were to ask her what she saw ten minutes ago, she probably wouldn't be able to answer. It never bothered her before; it made things easier, not having to focus, not needing to think too hard, like there's a switch on her brain always toggled off.

Yet, the more she considers now, the more that new, strange, itchy feeling weighing down on her chest begins to lighten. The pressure slowly goes away with each new possibility, and each new string of questions following behind it like little yellow ducklings waddling after their mother.

Alora hesitates, unsure of what she should do. She worries that if she keeps thinking, she'll become overwhelmed. Her thoughts will become too much, and soon she'll be drowning in them. She's never had questions she couldn't just search the internet and get an easy answer to. There's no website to tell her what the other person saw, what they were thinking; no way to understand what was going through their mind when they broke the quiet of the subway tram like shattering the glass on a window.

There are so many options, it makes Alora feel like her head is spinning. She can't decide if it's better or worse that there are no answers, no guidance, that it's just whatever she wants to think. Alora feels as though she's being used as bait on a giant fishing hook, being cast out to sea, not knowing what she'll find but only knowing she'll find something. The thought is scary, no rules, nothing to tell her if what she's coming up with is right or wrong, but the same thoughts are an easy escape from the boredom sitting beneath her skin.

So, despite the fear she feels of facing the unknown, she takes a deep breath and focuses on something else. She glances once more at the windows, but instead of just seeing the glass and the tunnel outside, she truly looks. She studies the way the flickering LED lights from the advertisements make the windows tint in hazy colors, and envisions it painted in other colors too, like a rainbow made of glass. She focuses on the tunnel outside, noticing how some of the lights along the path are darker than others, and lets herself wonder how they change the lightbulbs when one goes out.

And, when her focus moves to the floor, she studies the different stains left over from someone else's life, and wonders how old they are, and how they got there. Maybe one day, a mechanic came in with a cup of coffee and accidentally spilled a drop when the tram went too hard on a turn. Maybe a young mother was struggling to get a handle on her toddler, who forgot to charge their E-Device, and threw their juice during a tantrum.

By the end of her ride, Alora was so lost in her own world, making little stories about the things around her, she nearly missed her stop. It wasn't until the mechanical voice said, "Final call for stop 3346," that Alora sprang up and quickly advanced towards the exit before the doors closed. But it wasn't long after she made her way through the station, trying to find her way past people so lost in their electronics they couldn't even hear her politely say, "excuse me," that her mind began to wander to an easier distraction: her backup E-Device at home.

Instantly, her wonderings came to a halt like slamming on a car's brakes. Her brain, which had been swimming with imagination, quickly shut back off again as she traveled the familiar path back to her house. Now that her device was so close, and her mind was back on the normal schedule of AI videos, she had no more need to look at the world around her. Though with each step she took, she could almost feel the pestering breath of boredom hot on her heels.

Distraction Walking up the very familiar steps of her apartment building, Alora makes her way past the security drone hovering noiselessly in the entranceway and into one of the large, spacious elevators, which will take her up to the tenth floor without a hitch. The whole time, her mind only on one thing: *distraction*. She can't wait to feel the familiar cool touch of her spare E-Device and watch as the mechanical screen lights up with bright, artificial colors. By the time the elevator comes to a slow, steady stop, she has forgotten all about her peculiar subway ride home.

She rushes into the hallway, excited to be back online and reconnected with her usual life but suddenly stops in her tracks. Every door on floor ten looks exactly the same. Usually, the app on Alora's E-Device would tell her where to go, but without it, Alora feels hopelessly lost. She stands before the long hall, looking into the dull, repetitive space, and begins to feel uneasy.

She can't remember how far into the narrow passageway her door is, or how long it will take her to reach it. She's about to despair, afraid she'll never make it home, when the elevator behind her gives a small chime, and out walks a stranger. He's hunched over his screen, shoulders slumped as though burdened by a heavy, invisible weight, as focused on his E-Device as a dog would be on a squirrel. Alora quickly darts out of the way as the boy nearly collides with her! She watches, rather annoyed with the boy, as he follows his GPS into the hallway. He stops in front of a door not too far in, and after a moment, the door lets out a cheery jingle and opens automatically for the boy, who promptly disappears inside.

That's when Alora remembers the doors use facial recognition to open, meaning she isn't actually lost; she just has to find one that opens for her! The knowledge instantly makes Alora's dark cloud of despair evaporate, replaced with a sudden burst of determination. It takes Alora some trial and error, standing in front of every single door, and counting the seconds on her fingers, before moving to the next. Finally, after what felt like hours to her, but truthfully was only two minutes, Alora discovered her door. A large smile spread across her face as it belted out its familiar song and began to open. She can't remember ever feeling this happy to find her apartment before, but maybe doing it on her own, without her GPS, made it better somehow.

As she slips inside, Alora is greeted with a dimly lit space. The lights above her head buzz harshly, like a swarm of angry bees, and the windows that cover one wall are hidden behind large, dark, blackout curtains, stopping the warm, buttery sunlight from shining through. It's hard to see, and she has to squint as her eyes adjust. The whole apartment is cast in cold, low fluorescents that dance unnaturally with shadowy corners and slide off the walls. But Alora doesn't mind the dim, because it eliminates the chance of a glare disrupting the screens of her electronics. Besides, there isn't much to look at anyway. There are no family photos framed on the walls nor fake fruit displayed on the dining table. There are no funny vases filled with blooming flowers nor cluttered messes stashed discreetly into cupboards, no childhood art pinned to the fridge, and no strange porcelain figures livening the shelves. Even the walls themselves are bland, painted a sad, standard beige that clings desperately to the dark wooden accents and the paint lines are far too straight and perfect to be man-made.

There is absolutely nothing inside Alora's apartment that suggests someone actually lives there; it's bare bones. Even the smell of fresh linens and clean soap in the air around her is just a fabricated perfume, the same one that's used in every single building on the block. There is no sense of belonging, and certainly nothing special about it; the whole layout, color, and feel of the place is made the same as every other condo, apartment, and house in all of area 3346. Nonetheless, Alora does not see a problem with it; she doesn't understand what is missing.

As Alora navigates her way towards her room, a soft whir sounds from the kitchen, and she frowns as Ms.E46 glides down the hallway. Her structure is simple; her head is mounted on her body using a swivel post, allowing her to turn and look in any direction. Her body is a large metal cylinder, with interlocking parts so her 'waist' moves naturally. Her arms are the same, connected in the middle by a metal ball, letting the robot move as though she has elbows, and it is that same joint connection enabling her fingers to move. Instead of having feet, Ms.E46 just has a long post, with three large, spherical wheels on the bottom, like a little kid's tricycle. To finish her look, she's been painted a soft, metallic gray.

Alora's father built the robot by altering the generic code of a regular maid bot into something slightly more intelligent. Alora doesn't see him much anymore, despite living in the same space. On rare days, she might find him in the kitchen, pouring milk into a bowl, only to forget to pour the cereal in after it. Sometimes she passes him in the hallway, where he mutters an apology for being in her way with a voice that's rough from never being used.

After Alora's mother passed away when Alora was still an infant, her father locked himself away inside their old room. He made Ms.E46 raise her, giving the robot the command to keep her safe, happy, and healthy, while he kept tinkering with more electronics. So far, Ms.E46 is the only invention he's made that actually works.

"Welcome back, child number ten billion seven hundred eighty-two," sounds the robotic feminine voice from a speaker hidden somewhere inside of Ms.E46's chest. She used to call Alora by name, but after almost thirteen years, some of her memories have eroded.

"Thank you, E46," Alora answers instinctively, even though she knows the robot won't respond, and can't appreciate her words.

Just like Alora expected, the robot let out a puff of steam before answering, "Could not compute request".

Alora sighs, slightly irritated at the interruption. Usually, she doesn't mind Ms.E46's slightly bugged confusion; sometimes she even seeks it out, asking her random questions just to talk to *something*, and marvel at the string of outdated information and responses that sometimes feel like they hold emotion. But right now, it was keeping her from her E-Device.

"Please try …" Ms.E46 starts but is quickly interrupted.

"Dismissed," Alora says curtly, not wanting to listen to the robot's usual speech.

Ms.E46 pauses for a moment, calculating the new order, before bobbing her head in a jerky, unnatural mimic of nodding. She then spins quickly on her wheels, generating a flawless half circle, and rolls back in the direction of the small kitchen where she had probably been preparing dinner.

The moment the robot is gone, Alora once more rushes towards her room. She stops in front of it, waiting impatiently for the door to recognize her face and let her in, before dashing inside the second the opening is large enough. She throws herself onto her bed, the only piece of furniture in the room other than an incredibly old, worn-down nightstand placed loyally beside her. On top of the rickety wooden stand is her spare E-Device, plugged into a massive, gray cord that's wrapped around one of the nightstand's legs before disappearing beneath her bed.

It's a larger model than the handheld ones. This E-Device has an outward keyboard and a larger screen, but it still has all the power of the smaller ones, and that's all Alora cared about. Perched, folded neatly, waiting for her to use it and dive back into the shelter of mindless entertainment. Alora wastes no more time, propping herself up in bed with her back against a large, doughy pillow. She sits with her legs crossed, making the perfect stand for the device, before gently removing it from its charger and placing it into her lap.

As she unfolds it, a sudden spike of joy lights her up from the inside out, and she smiles brightly at the old friend. Its screen turns on with a kindly chime; one that's more familiar to Alora than the air in her lungs. The second she unlocks it, ads explode onto the screen, bright colors, neon lights, and odd, animated characters flood her screen and fill her brain. She watches a few, vaguely recalling a few of the characters she's looking at, before powering up the ad blocker and watching them all disappear with a satisfying pop.

She didn't bother clicking on the pinned tab of her online school; it is an old, outdated website that hadn't been updated for decades. Everyone under eighteen is 'required' to complete it, but AI does all the work for her. The second a new module is posted, AI generates a response quicker than Alora can blink and turns it in a split second later with a perfect score.

So instead, she finds her favorite website, a better version of what was once called 'social media' a hundred years ago. It's all been combined onto one site, easy to navigate, and even easier to get lost in. If Alora could, she'd spend days on it, maybe even months, just scrolling through videos. But, of course, there were days, like today, when they ran out of groceries, and she would have to eventually visit the World Market to order their next shipment of food.

Now that she's home, though, Alora is excited to sink back into the haze of doing absolutely nothing. Yet, the more she searches, trying to dive into the pool and sink to the bottom, surrounded by blissful sounds and random fake clips, the less excited she feels. She finds herself glancing around the room between seconds, eyes scurrying as if searching for something else, something more entertaining.

Confused, Alora switches to a new tab, flipping through movies she's already watched, and the ones she hasn't. Each description is read aloud to her as she hovers over their icon, the automated AI voice pouring out of the device's speakers and into her ears, but she doesn't find a single one that sounds good to her. Alora speaks a new phrase, watching the words appear across the screen's search bar. She looks through tens of hundreds of thousands of games, every genre, every play style, and yet, nothing.

She feels empty and completely unfulfilled, and, to her horror, the feeling that followed her from the subway tram, up the steps of her apartment, into the elevator, down the hall, and stalked just a few steps behind all the way into her room, is back. The emotion is reaching for her, trying to get her back into its clutches.

Alora urgently messages her chatbot, trying really hard to describe what she's feeling, but the response it generated was even more frustrating. It told her she was most likely bored, and the only way to fix it was to distract herself, but that's all she's been trying to do! No matter how many times she regenerates the response, it always tells her the same thing, over and over, as repetitive as the design of the hallway outside and the apartment complexes lined up in neat perfect rows beyond that.

It made her frown, tears pricking at the corners of her eyes, as boredom weighed heavily on her once again. She finally caves, turning on the first ASMR video that comes up on her recommended list, before delicately putting the E-Device back onto the nightstand. She pulls the covers up and over her head like the emotion was a monster she could hide away from and tossed and turned for hours before finally settling into a restless sleep.

3

Hope Alora awoke to the buttery light of the sun, trying to stretch beneath the heavy curtains of her bedroom window. The gentle sunbeams fail to reach her across the cold floor, though not for a lack of trying. The whispers of a stranger's customized avatar play loudly from the E-Device on her bedstand. The original video she put on while trying to fall asleep was long gone, lost in the sea of perfectly replicated, matching videos designed to keep Alora comfortably asleep. But, for once, the ASMR didn't work.

Alora tossed and turned all night, occasionally startling awake, trying to *try* harder than ever before to fall back to sleep. Something plagued her usual slumber. Where there was usually nothing but a dark, endless void until she woke, there had been pleasant colors swirling behind her eyelids as she slept. It was as though watching a movie, but her eyes were fully closed, and the plot was much more confusing and unusual than her regular shows. Even more odd, Alora seemed to forget everything that had happened every time she opened her eyes. These strange, sleepy visions left her dazed and confused, struggling to hold on to the story that immediately flew from her fingers like dust in the wind.

She has no idea what time it is as she sits up in bed, rubbing the sleep from her eyes and blinking away the last blurry remnants. It doesn't matter much since she never has anything to do anyway. Alora's reluctant to leave the warm haven of her covers; usually, she'd nap for hours more, or even days on end, but now she feels so restless. She simply has to move or else her head might explode! Perhaps the new feeling that followed her all the way home from the tram is what made her mind dance with light while she slept, but Alora doesn't want to dwell on it. Hallucinations were not one of the descriptors given when she'd looked up what boredom is, and the information online is clearly never wrong.

She swings her legs over the side of her bed and hops down. Goosebumps rise along her arms, and a tiny shiver races up her spine at the cold kiss of the wooden floor against her feet, but the sensors quickly adjust it to fit her temperature needs, heating beneath each soft footstep. Alora makes her way to the bathroom, letting the robotic arm brush her teeth, style her hair, and get her ready as it always does. Then, she heads down the hallway, following the alluring scent of whatever Ms.E46 cooked earlier.

She wasn't even a foot into the kitchen before the robot sounded her routine, "Good morning," her voice never changing pitch or tone. Ms.E46 doesn't need to look to know it's Alora who is scooting out one of the two chairs at the dining table, or who mumbles a quiet, "Good morning," in return. The robot has enough sensors to recognize people not just by look, but by temperature, heartbeat, and footsteps.

"You sound tired, child number ten billion seven hundred eighty two," Ms.E46 announces without pausing her breakfast preparations. "Have you fallen under the weather?" she asks without concern.

Emotions were never a part of E46's upgrades; it goes way beyond her model and has been known to crash systems anyway. "Your temperature has not risen and your heartbeat is regular," the robot continues, "I may be in need of upgrades to fully assess ..."

"I'm not sick!" Alora corrects.

"I see. How may I be of assistance?"

Alora knows Ms.E46 feels no true care, but, in her eyes, that's always been *its* way of asking what's wrong, like the old robot was trying to work around her programming barriers.

Still, Alora hesitates, torn between telling the robot her problems and just letting them be. She wants to solve them, of course, but she's tried everything her AI companion suggested, every distraction she could think of, and an out of touch machine like Ms.E46 would probably be even more unhelpful.

Practically desperate Alora feels boredom crawling beneath her skin even now, waiting for the second it gets just a little too quiet, or a little too repetitive, to strike again. "I'm bored!" Alora blurts out, "And I don't know what to do, I've tried everything!"

The robot pauses its movements, seeming to ponder for a moment as she computes the new information, slower than any usual search engine, before beginning to spit out the same spiel as the AI Alora did last night. Alora is about to give up hope completely when Ms.E46 finally mentions something new: *picking up a hobby*.

The new words replace the AI's suggestion of just using more distractions, which means Ms.E46 might have actually found something new for Alora to try. She sits up fast in her seat, suddenly leaning in, letting her elbows rest heavily on the table as she places her head in her hands. "What types of hobbies?" Alora asks quickly, interrupting the robot, who struggles to keep up with the sudden new direction.

A steady whir sounds from Ms.E46's head as she calculates the new question as quickly as she can. Alora has never had a hobby, though she knows what they are. Just like her dad and his obsession with creating new robots, though she always found it to seem like a waste of time, and an incredibly tiring one at that. Yet it could work as a new distraction, now that Ms.E46 mentions it.

"Browsing the internet, testing out new media platforms, or visiting many of the millions of game sites programmed into all E-Devices are good hobbies," E46 drones.

Alora's smile slips from her face; those are all things she's already tried and haven't worked. She sighs heavily, and a frown tugs at her lips until she's pouting, melting into the dining room chair, her worry already starting to come back, now two times stronger than before.

"You are unsatisfied," Ms.E46 acknowledges like a sudden beacon of light in an oncoming storm, "I will search for a more satisfactory answer, one moment please," sounds the robot's voice, before the familiar hum returns.

Alora sits stunned for a moment. No program has ever offered to find another response, not any of the newer models anyway. They always seem to spit out the same thing, no matter how Alora phrases the question. It cuts through her dismay, her heart soaring inside her chest as she waits with bated breath for Ms.E46 to be done reprocessing.

It seems to take an eternity, but not long enough to dampen Alora's newfound hope; in fact, her hope only grows with each second that ticks by. The anticipation makes her head swim, but finally, the gentle sounds coming from Ms.E46 are replaced with her monotone voice, "There are many hobbies that do not involve electronics."

Alora practically burst from her seat like a rocket in her joy.

Ms.E46 continues, "People used to spend time doing more creative tasks, such as crocheting, sports, plays, painting, drawing, reading, writing, and more."

Alora quickly asks E46 to print the information out so that she can remember. E46 easily complies, printing out a singular piece of paper from her cylinder body and passing it across the table to Alora. She takes it from the robot's cold, mechanical fingers and reads it over a couple of times, just looking at the words, at the different hobbies, at the suddenly vast amount of new things she can try.

Once again, Alora feels the boredom seeping away, replaced by a glowing yellow excitement, a feeling blooming like a flower in her heart, and brings the smile instantly back to her face, this time so wide it makes her cheeks hurt.

"These are old hobbies, outdated and deemed inefficient compared to the modern advancements of our new technical society," Ms.E46 warns, but Alora doesn't pay attention, not anymore, not when the robot says something that goes directly against her happiness.

"Thank you, E46," Alora says absent-mindedly, still staring in amazement at the list clutched in her hands.

The robot stalls before saying she does not need a thank you and cannot appreciate the sentiment. For once, Alora doesn't mind, and it seems as though the room around her has gotten brighter, as if even the colors themselves were excited about having a new solution to Alora's boredom problem.

The robot gently loads two plates with eggs, sausages, and perfectly buttered toast. She sets it down in front of Alora, careful not to disturb the girl, before wheeling away to find Alora's father. Yet Alora is so thrilled she nearly forgets to eat, and when she does, her mind is wandering so far into the possibilities she barely finishes half of the breakfast before dashing back towards her room, leaving her plate to grow cold on the table.

4

Excitement The second the door opens, Alora rushes into her room with the printed paper of new hobbies cradled close to her chest like a lifeline. A newfound purpose thrums through her veins, a promise of freedom from the foul emotion that's been haunting her for far too long. She hurriedly sets down the now slightly crumpled piece of paper on her pillow and reaches immediately for her E-Device and settles onto the edge of her bed. Her back already aches from sitting up straight, but she's far too excited to lie down fully or find a more comfortable position, as she pulls the E-Device's screen open.

Alora whispers her password into the hidden microphone that's always on and always listening, waiting for her to speak her commands, and watches in delight as the device unlocks. Her fingers are already swiping across the large screen, not bothering with the massive trackpad that takes up half of the barely used keyboard. She's determined now, unwilling to be tortured by boredom anymore, and ready to try practically anything to get it to go away. She's not sure why it started, but she's certain she will find a way to end it.

She glances at the paper on her pillow, whispering the words to her E-Device and watching as the screen lights up with results. The first one, crocheting, comes up with thousands of images. It's not as many as she hoped for, not nearly as much as would come up from modern-day hobbies, like video games, or AI art makers, but she isn't deterred. What greets her is a large variety of items formed from soft, looping thread. The amount of colors in each piece puts her entire apartment to shame; in fact, it makes the usual grays of metal, normal beiges, and common woody browns look almost sad in comparison. Alora scrolls through pictures of blue fuzzy elephants, multi-colored coasters, huge, intricate blankets made with the colors of sunsets, and so many more.

She's so engrossed in the images she doesn't realize whole minutes have passed her by. The colors alone are stunning, beautiful, and bright in a way that wasn't artificial like her screen or dulled and souring like every building and machine she passes. That alone is enough to put her in a trance. Something in her chest tightens, and a lump begins to form in her throat, heavy and hard to swallow around. Her eyes water, sudden tears springing up into the corners.

Alora isn't sad; in fact, she's so happy looking at the crocheted creations she doesn't know what to do with herself. A smile, real and warm, forms on her face as she keeps scrolling to find out more. Yet, all the videos she glances at are old, the graphics aren't nearly life-like enough, and the crocheting patterns seem difficult for her to copy. Even the easiest ones are confusing to her, and she doesn't know where to find the right tools for such a task.

With a heavy heart, Alora decides to move down to the next outdated hobby on the list.

She whispers 'sports' into her device, and millions of videos pour onto her screen. It's a much more promising amount compared to crocheting, but, as she looks through the videos, she doesn't feel the same pull. In fact, her smile even fades a little. Every sport seems to require being outside, which is something no one nowadays ever wants to do. It's hot in some places, and too cold in others. It would be too much effort just to stand the temperatures alone. Not to mention Alora doesn't even know any real people besides her dad, and most of the sports seem to require at least two.

Besides, the fields and snow that show up in these sports don't exist anymore. Now, most of the parks and yards in the area are made of green plastic, and the snow that falls in the winter is just computer-made goo. All of it is synthetic; none of it is natural like Alora sees in the videos. Her eyebrows knit together in something oddly like concern, as she realizes the difference, but she doesn't dwell on it for long. Already bored with sports and not wanting to get any aspect of a hobby wrong, she skips to the next one.

Alora is surprised to read 'movies' rank as the third interest. Don't get her wrong, Alora is a fan of movies, even though they aren't quite as fast-paced as her usual videos. She remembers, very vaguely, when she was young, Ms.E46 played animated movies for her whenever she was fussy. It was a part of the robots protocol, 'how to care for toddlers'. Even now, she indulges in them every once in a while. The nostalgia of watching one is too great to brush off, even if they're all too long for her to finish. However, the idea of creating one herself is a little confusing. It's an odd feeling, realizing she can produce something she's enjoyed for so long, just like her father with his robots. Plus, unlike the other two pastimes she's looked over, this one is something she actually understands! She decides to give it a go, excited to try something new.

"It shouldn't be too hard," Alora quietly says to encourage herself, "I've watched so many movies already."

Nonetheless, Alora quickly realizes it isn't as easy as she thought it was going to be. Alora finds herself hanging upside down from her bed, her hands splaying across the cold floor, hair dangling and resting in a pool of waves beneath her. She thought that maybe, going upside down and hanging from her bed would give her some ideas.

Her new findings didn't change what she's been staring at this whole time: the smooth, tannish walls in her bedroom, the bland white ceiling, and the deep, black curtain that clings to her window. Her bed covers are black, the same as the curtain, and the door connecting to her bathroom is painted the same dull white as the ceiling, meaning nothing in her space is remotely inspiring.

Her frustration only grows; the bulky and uncomfortably restless feeling has already returned with it, and still, the only things she can come up with are just as dull as everything around her. No one wants to watch a movie about the different shades of beige in someone's hallway versus their bedroom, or a day in the life of a maid robot. None of them hold a candle to the movies she's seen; it barely lets out a puff of smoke next to others' blazing fires.

Finally, something different catches her eye. The sun. It's still trying to struggle its way through the crack in the curtains, but the slivers that do get through leak across her floor with a mellow shine. Where the sunlight meets the dark wood, the surface seems to lighten into a softer, warmer brown. The contrast is so striking, Alora can actually see the patterns hidden inside the oak. Her eyes trace the small area of light, nearly transfixed for a moment, before a new idea finally sparks!

The deep brown allure makes Alora think of rich rivers of chocolate flowing through a land of candy, sweet and perfect and wonderful as can be. She sits up far too fast, making her vision blacken for just a moment as she tries to right herself. Then she just as speedily remembers there's already a movie about such a magical place, something she had watched when she was little, but doesn't remember fully anymore.

Alora groans, flopping back amidst her pillows. Feeling defeated, she reaches over to her E-Device and pauses the music streaming from its speakers. She wasn't paying attention to what was playing anyway. Her focus quieted every distraction. Yet, despite all her effort, nothing she could come up with was original.

She looks over to the E-Devices screen, which seems to be beckoning her closer like it's welcoming her home. Her gut twists at the thought, and she nearly feels sick at the idea of turning back towards electronics to help her complete the one task she thought she could do on her own. But the promise of simple easy ideas have her pulling it back towards her before she can even think about it. "Give me movie ideas," she demands, voice shaking slightly, into the E-Device.

AI responds to her eagerly, proudly presenting her with its own idea in less than a second. But, as Alora skims over the words, she can't help but realize it sounds familiar. She quickly looks it up, and sure enough, the idea AI gave her is also already a movie. "Give me an *original* movie idea," Alora tries again.

AI apologizes and corrects itself swiftly before sending her another small paragraph. Yet, once again, the idea feels far too familiar, and, when she searches for it, it pops up once more as an already existing movie.

"That isn't original!" Alora shouts, her frustration shifting into anger, bubbling up inside, fueled by the fear of failure and the sudden realization that something isn't right.

AI recalculates, generating piece after piece, but each one already exists; each transcription AI frames as *new* is pre-made, or already a part of a show, movie, or some sort of media. To Alora's dismay, no matter how she phrases it, what words she uses, or what genre she suggests, every movie concept AI generates all turn out the same way; sharing the same plot devices, the same underlying story, and even some of the characters it mentioned windup being repeated in other movies.

While Alora looks up each and every 'original idea', she begins to map out a truth she's never noticed before. A constant, never-ending, never stopping, retelling of the same few stories. Movies that end the same, have the same characters, whose 'new rising actors' are actually people who have already been in hundreds of other movies. No matter what comes up, it always seems to double back on itself as if they've grown from the same, predictable root.

After nearly an entire hour of fighting with the system, of searching across numerous platforms, of scanning high and low for one thing that doesn't match everything else, Alora just sits and stares blankly at her E-Device's screen. Her heart is racing like she's just walked up a flight of stairs instead of taking the elevator. Her palms are wet with sweat, and her face is rough with dried tears. She can't help but feel as though she's just stumbled into something that's been buried for decades and was never meant to be uncovered.

Her excitement shifted, snuffed like a candle wick, burnt out by quickly drying wax. It's replaced with dread, which fills the pit of her stomach, as she realizes everything; every movie, every video, every show, and even the little skits she's watched her whole life, have been nearly the same thing. They're about the same recycled topics, or hold the same opinions, or contain generic generated perfection.

As Alora stares without truly seeing, swallowing hard against a suddenly dry throat, the sun behind the curtains is setting, mocking her with time that's running out.

5

Determination Alora's revitalized heart is racing so fast she's afraid it's going to run straight out of her chest and never come back. The soft weight of her E-Device rubbing against the fabric of her pants suddenly feels too heavy, and she pushes it off of her lap like it's burning her. It settles onto the bed beside her, screen still glowing, bright and taunting.

Alora feels as though all of the air in her room has left, leaving her lungs empty no matter how hard she breathes. Her feet are moving before she even thinks about where she's going. All she knows is she has to go somewhere and get away from the sinking feeling in her gut, like a rock-filled sock thrown into a deep river.

Her feet thud softly against the wooden floor as she rushes out of her room, pushing past Ms.E46, who calls out behind her, "You should not go outside without shoes. It is unsafe, and you could contract a multitude of illnesses."

Alora barely hears her warning. She probably would've ignored it anyway over the sound of the blood rushing in her ears.

She shoots out into the apartment hall-way, feeling the uncomfortable carpet sink slightly under her feet as she heads towards the elevators. The subtle chime as it reaches her floor and the doors sliding open is lost in the blur of her alarm. Every moment makes the panic in Alora's chest spike until she's breathing heavy. She folds her arms tight across her chest as she walks into the elevator, as if she's holding herself together, and the cool shift between the squishy hallway carpet and the cold metal floor sends a shiver up from her ankles to the base of her neck.

She knows where she's going now, nerves making her feel sick to her stomach, but she has to see it. She's going outside, to look truly for once, to see for herself just how repetitive and artificial the world around her became while she's been too distracted with her screen to look around and notice.

On the way, Alora stops at nearly every floor. She finds what she expected, but it only makes her feel sicker, flushed with a tense, anxious sheen of sweat. Each floor looks the same, not a thing out of place. The carpet is cut the same, the pattern is in the same place, and the walls are the same colors with no sign of chips, stains, or even fading. Alora even pauses, takes whole seconds to count how many little diamonds are in the carpet, every time it's fourteen without fail.

When she finally reaches the first floor, she already feels exhausted. Strung tight like a bow, Alora can feel how tense the muscles in her back are, and her hands keep clenching and unclenching by her sides, with a restless, uneasy energy. Still, she refuses to stop, no matter how much a part of her longs to just go back to the dark safety of her room, back to her E-Device, and just wait out her boredom.

Instead, she cuts across the lobby of the apartment building. The security drone pays her no mind, hovering in the middle of the large space, camera swiveling back and forth as if tracking a thousand miniature movements Alora could never hope to notice. Down here, the light of the setting sun reaches through the glass front doors with fingers outstretched, casting the whole space with a subtle glow. It hurts Alora's eyes; she's never faced the sun directly before. Even the subdued, setting light, far darker than the screen of her E-Devices, makes her eyes water. But she pushes forward anyway, eyes squinting against the sunbeams, needing to discover, to see, and she isn't intent on stopping until she's confirmed what she's always known deep down.

She bursts outside, throwing the front doors open, and feeling the warm, rough concrete of the sidewalk against the bare skin of her feet. It burns for a moment, shocking Alora, as she had forgotten what heat felt like. All buildings are kept at the same temperature, even the tram is the same, but the sun-warmed cement doesn't follow any rules. She got used to it after a moment, the heat turning into something comforting and nice that made her want to lie down and soak up the rest of the coziness before the sun fully set. Alora never considered doing such a thing before.

Without her E-Device in hand, or her mind wandering to ideas of distractions, everything around her seemed more intense, more real. It is as if she is waking up from a very long sleep and is seeing how the world's changed around her after all the time that's passed. Even just looking down at the sidewalk beneath her brought new things for Alora to see, the narrow cracks in the sidewalk forming miniature canyons for the tiny ants to trudge along, or the lost items littering the path. She's shocked by the amount alone, fallen keys, dropped wallets, and miles upon miles of carelessly strewn cans and garbage bags being tossed around by the soft breeze rustling through the fake, plastic grass.

Alora has never noticed any of this before. Usually, with her music blasting in her ears and her eyes focused solely on random games played for a couple of minutes before finding a new one, she wouldn't have been able to hear the way the wind runs its fingers through the sky. Much less the feel of trash crunching beneath her shoes, or the tiny bugs marching past her.

But that isn't what she's focusing on now, though she surely wants to get lost in all of it later; she still has to settle the pit formed in her stomach. So, Alora's gaze lifts, hesitantly, to follow the path of buildings perfectly lined up around her in neat, uniform rows.

She'd never realized on her route back from the tram station just how many buildings she weaved through to get to hers. Alora doesn't even remember memorizing the way, only knowing it like the back of her hand, able to follow it without pausing the dart of her fingers across a screen. But now, staring at the rows of apartment buildings lined up in front of her, she doesn't feel a sense of awe, but instead, a swirling, dizzying fright. As far as her eyes can see, in both directions, from behind her, to in front of her, and from her left, to her right, is the same building. It's as if the robots that built it copied and pasted each one across the world, or at least, until it disappeared from view.

Alora is half tempted to walk the length of the sidewalk, to see how far she can go until she finds something that stands out. Even the large, metal billboards that shoot up from the ground like artificial trees and blink with the lights of ads playing nonstop on a silent screen appear every five complexes, without fail. They play the same ads too, ones that look outdated now, with bright colors, muted, and bleached by the sun. It's probably from years ago, and no one had bothered to tear it down or replace it.

It's like the world's stopped, frozen in place, moving neither forward nor backward, just repeating the same few days over and over in a tedious mind-numbing loop. The dis-covery only confirms what Alora realized back up in her room: in her entire life, nothing different has ever happened. No stone out of place, no blade of fake plastic grass cut slightly askew. No building shorter than the other, no faulty advertisements that don't land right, or blackouts like she's seen in movies. Everything's smooth and shiny and perfect, looking new and yet growing so entirely old and, with every moment she spends actually looking, more distressingly *fake*.

Alora stands there for a long time, at the entrance of her apartment building, just staring and taking it all in. She doesn't know whether she should be comforted by the fact she was right or disturbed by the truth that's been so blazingly obvious she might as well have had someone whispering it in her ear twenty-four seven. Either way, the weight in her stomach eases, and the tension in her muscles bleeds out into something softer. It isn't defeat, far from it, if anything, this discovery makes her want to fight more. Not just against boredom this time, but for herself, for something new, for her to prove she can do something no robot can do.

When the sun finally sets, and the beautiful, tangerine oranges and light hazy pinks fade into deep purples and inky blacks, Alora turns to head back inside. She takes the stairs instead of the elevator, the strain making her legs burn slightly as she walks all the way to the tenth floor, but it makes pride sing in her chest when she reaches her door without any help.

She slips inside the house and turns on all the lights along the way, changing the low, buzzing fluorescents into blinding bulbs that burn bright. They don't bring the same radiant heat as the sun, but at least she can finally see the space around her, even if it's as bland and annoyingly perfect as everything else.

Ms.E46, who has never dealt with the lights being fully on before, comes urgently wheeling around the corner. "It is impolite to keep the lights on so bright at night; it could awaken the neighbors. Make sure you are keeping up with your manners," the robot scolds in the same tone she uses to praise, offer advice, or ask about Alora's day.

Alora just nods, pretending to listen to E46, and escapes once more into her room. She hops onto her E-Device again, but this time, she refuses to get distracted. She won't be deterred by how hard something looks or how unpopular it seems. She's going to find something to do that'll let her never touch another screen again. The thought thrills her and pushes her to keep going. She grabs the list of hobbies from where she had left it, moving down the list with a new speed. The less she spends looking at the screen of her E-Device, the better.

She searches for 'paintings' and 'artworks', but, to her ever-growing frustration, she finds AI has already gotten to that too. A past time, once something for people to create, on things called canvases, with brushes dipped in color or chunks of wax, or even charcoal, has been turned fully digital and transformed by uncreative untalented robots. Alora's jaw clenches with fury; an anger she's never felt before in her life crashes over her like an ocean wave amid a storm.

She keeps going, keeps looking, the need to create flowing through her veins like the very blood that keeps her heart pumping.

That's when she accidentally types two searches at the same time in her haste, 'writing' and 'book', smooshed together into one word. The mistake leads her to a miracle. A notebook. A thing people can use to write with their own two hands. No typing, no whispering into an electronic, no mindless generating of a story that's been told and retold millions of times.

Alora's found her hobby.

6

Freedom Alora stares for a long moment at the multitude of notebooks on her E-Device's blaringly bright screen. The folded-up pieces of paper are stuffed neatly into protective covers and dyed as many colors as the world itself holds. They're completely void of everything electronic; anything written inside can't be read by text-to-speech, whispered into creation, or typed in by lazy fingers. Everything inside is put there, almost magically, by a person's own two hands.

'How to write in a notebook', Alora clumsily types into her E-Device, which immediately gives her multiple ways to type on a keyboard. It's annoying, as if the machine itself is trying to stop Alora from chasing her newfound dream. She scrolls down, reaches the end of the first page of websites, and continues to the next. She can't stop now. Alora won't let herself slow down until she finds what she needs.

Alora's hands tremble each time she has to scroll further, reading each website's short title thoroughly to make sure she doesn't miss the answer she desperately needs. There's a yearning in her chest and a tug at her heart with each swipe of her fingers against the touchpad on the keyboard. Each time her heart beats, it feels like a demand, a need to make a creation all her own. An idea, once a reality in the past, that only her mind and her hands can make come to life.

It isn't until she reaches the very bottom of the third page, that she finds an article that even mentions actual physical notebooks. She clicks on the link without a second thought, knowing there wouldn't be a virus on such an old site E-Devices haven't already been trained to deal with. The website itself is poorly made, or, at least, poorly made in Alora's time. Maybe it was made by an actual person, too, instead of the professionally AI-created games and blogs Alora sees now.

The format it uses is the one indie games nowadays try to reference, and the colors are bright and exciting rather than the standard off-whites and minimalist, barely incorporated primary colors. To Alora, though, that gives it charm; scrolling through the loud, vibrant website is like drinking a cold glass of water after waking up from a long, slightly uncomfortable nap.

The site itself is supposed to be used to guide mothers to teach their children how to write with an object Alora never saw before: a pencil. From the video provided, which is so low quality her E-Device has trouble running it, it appears to be a long, thin wooden stick, with a strikingly yellow casing. It reminds her almost of the protective cover on her handheld E-Device before she lost it, but it definitely wasn't as sturdy. At the tip of the pencil is something gray and sharp, and when pressed down into the notebook, it leaves heavy black lines behind, forming the letters almost as if by magic!

Alora watches the video once, twice, three times, her eyes wide and filled with unabashed fascination. Something pulls at her, trying to absorb her into the video, as she watches a person, by hand, create letters on a piece of paper, putting more effort into each line of each letter than she has ever put into anything in her whole life. She yearns to do the same, a bone-deep aching sort of need spreads from her fingertips to her arms and through her chest until it wraps around her heart and fills her lungs like it's the air she needs to breathe.

With this video playing on loop, she barely takes note of the way it begins to darken even further outside her room, or Ms.E46's robotic voice calling for her to eat the dinner that's been waiting for her. All she can see in this moment, through eyes watering with salty tears of awe, is her future. It is as if something inside her has changed and Alora knows suddenly this is what she wants to do, what she *needs* to do, and what she's always meant to discover.

In a world filled with electronics and distractions, and fake maddening perfection, Alora can finally break free. Just as a butterfly emerges from its cocoon or a bird takes its first flight, Alora is going to write. She's going to create, to foresee a world of her own and fill it with all the colors of a sunset, and all the admiration of a past that wasn't taken over by smog and pollution and robots to do all the thinking for her.

Alora is going to be free.

She searches for her favorite shopping website, filled with basically everything one could ask for. She knows no real store sells notebooks anymore, so she turns to the section where people sell old artifacts or 'rare' findings that have been passed on or they just happen across. Maybe from a great-grandmother's keepsakes. They could be from the last few antique stores still around, before they shut down for good. Most people have already stopped caring about what happened before and what'll happen next.

Regardless of how they found it, or where, Alora is unwavering in her search for a notebook and pencils; even if it's the last one in all of existence, she'll be the one to find it. To her surprise and utter delight, it doesn't take long to discover someone practically giving away a notebook and an entire pack of pencils. The caption says, "Ancient wood twigs, yellow color, chewy pink ends, and a square of weird, lined, dried-out cleaning wipes", below it, the total price of only five dollars. Five dollars, and Alora could hold her entire dream in her hands.

It makes her a little sad to see it priced so cheap. If only the seller knew what they had, the wonder and the liberty they held in their hands when taking the pictures for the website. Alora purchases it quickly, used to things selling out rather fast, though it's not as though anyone else is going to swipe it up from under her nose; she doubts anyone even knows what this is anymore.

She receives an automated message almost instantly, thanking her for her purchase and unfortunately, the person she ordered from doesn't pay the website premium, meaning she will have to go and pick it up herself. The thought for once doesn't annoy her; she's actually excited to go outside again tomorrow and feel the sun on her skin and breathe in the fresh outside air.

When she finally leaves her room to eat dinner, Ms.E46 notes Alora 'appears happier'. Alora grins from ear to ear at the robot, "I found a new hobby!" she announces.

Ms.E46 gives her a monotone, unemotional congratulations before rolling off to do more chores. Usually, that would bother Alora, but tonight she's far too excited. Tomorrow, she'll get her notebook and start her life for the first time.

7

Curiosity The next morning Alora experiences a gentle lull of excitement as she takes her time to complete her usual morning routine. The mirror in her connecting bathroom, which is usually lit up with beauty ads and timers for how long she should wash her hands and brush her teeth, is now turned completely off. Instead of heavy artificial lights and fake greetings from hundreds of AI-created influencer morning routines, Alora sees only her reflection, and she can't stop grinning at herself. Her smile stretches ear to ear, and she's elated by her ability to go a whole morning without reaching for an electronic device, blasting music, or shoving her headphones into her ears and turning on background noise.

She's never actually taken the time to stop like this, to look at herself in the mirror, or to think through the steps of brushing her teeth. To put the effort into living instead of rushing through her life with videos playing mindlessly on loop to keep her occupied. Now, the seconds, which usually seem to fly by fast, days bleeding into each other and wasted more and more with each scroll from one video to the next, have slowed. It's a sudden shift, a speeding car slamming on its brakes when a deer jumps into its path, but Alora welcomes it with open arms.

She's beginning to realize it's almost peaceful in a way, to be fully unplugged. The feeling is like she's truly breathing deeply for the first time, appreciating the air that's rushing through her lungs and keeping her alive. Today is the first morning since she can remember when she's present enough to smell the mint of her toothpaste, and to feel each pass of her hairbrush smoothing through her long locks. When she finally emerges from her bedroom, she finds that, although this morning felt much slower than usual, she's made it out of bed nearly an entire hour earlier than normal, which only makes her feel more giddy. Things only seem to get better with every second she spends focusing on the physical instead of the artificial!

As Alora makes her way to the kitchen, she pauses in the hallway, closing her eyes tightly and sucking in the sweet mouth-watering aroma of muffins baking in the oven. Ms.E46 usually makes a batch in the morning, but Alora never wakes up early enough to see it, or often finds herself not caring enough to pull herself out of her digital trance, to get them while they're warm, much less not yet out of the oven.

"Just another perk of not using my E-Device," Alora whispers to herself, her joy melting out into her voice until it sounds as cheery as she feels.

On the short trip to the kitchen, there's a spring in Alora's step and a brightness all about her that's replaced her usual distracted feet-dragging and zoned-out expression. Before she sits down at the dining table, Alora makes her way to the window on the far wall of the room and, in one heave, throws open the blackout curtains. The warm morning sun floods in, reaching for Alora and wrapping her up in a hug she melts into. She watches as the room instantly brightens, the sun's rays filling the space much nicer than the faintly buzzing overhead lights.

"If it is too dark, I can turn up the lights' brightness," Ms.E46 chimes in from where she stands by the oven, her robotic voice crackling through her worn-down speakers. Her TV-like head reflects the glare of the natural light, casting spots onto the far wall. Alora watches in astonishment, eyes wide, smile bright and shining, like a little kid on Christmas morning. Which is exactly how Alora feels, as if she's young again, everything new and big and magnificent. Back before electronics seized her whole life. Before she surrendered to spending most of her days locked in her bedroom, a prisoner to the screen she would soon hold like treasure in her hands.

But not now, not anymore, Alora is sure she won't let herself go back to that life. She won't have to, because by the end of this day, she's going to have a notebook in hand and stories flooding each page, that she's sure of.

"I didn't open the window because it's dark, I just wanted some sun," Alora corrects E46, hopeful that when she opens the rest of the windows, the robot won't try to turn all the overhead lights on to max power as well. She's not sure she can handle the amount of strained buzzing the lights will produce on the high setting; they already sound like beehives on low!

Ms.E46 pauses, no doubt trying to find an unemotional, robotic reason for Alora's answer. "The sun is very good for Vitamin D, something most humans are currently lacking." Ms.E46 finally concludes, before turning stiffly back towards the oven, her job of providing required interaction with Alora now complete for the day.

It doesn't take long for the muffins to come out of the oven, and Alora hurries to snatch multiple out of the pan at once, reveling in the warm bread beneath her fingers. E46 warns, without much urgency and absence of care, to be cautious when eating the muffins before they have time to cool. Alora nods along, but the second E46 wheels a small plate towards Alora's father's room, she's practically stuffing handfuls of them down her throat. The first few bites burn her tongue just lightly, and she almost regrets not listening to the robot, but she can't help it! She's too happy this morning, feeling refreshed for once and finally having something to look forward to; it's nearly too much for her to bear!

When Alora finally heads out the door, eager to get to the pick-up location, she stops occasionally on her walk to the tram station to admire the scenery around her. Unfortunately, most of it looks nearly identical, except for the multi-colored trash lying around, and the occasional billboard showing a separate string of ads than the others, which sort of feels like finding a rare creature in one of Alora's favorite online games. Regardless, each small crack in the sidewalks or slightly miscolored blade of plastic grass is enough to hold her fascination. She's never truly looked at the world she lives in, and, although it nearly frightened her half to death yesterday, she can't help the sense of awe it brings to her now. Especially because every sight looks the same, every building replicated and colors matched, just spurs her on even more.

Mostly, she looks up at the sky, which is still uncontrollable by AI. She'd seen it once in an incredibly ancient movie, and also in some of the videos that showed up when she was searching 'sports'. That's how she discovered the sky was once blue. It's hard for her to visualize, especially now, staring at the muted hazy brown layer of smoke covering most of the heavens like one thick cloud. The sun pushes through, but Alora can only fantasize how beautiful it could've been to see it without the smog. She bets the sunsets would be a million times more beautiful than the one she watched yesterday. Then again, when the only colors she usually sees are overedited ones cast through screens or the dull beiges and overcompensating whites of her home, any natural color is exceedingly beautiful to Alora.

The closer she gets to the tram station, the more people flood the space around her. They're all on their mobile E-Devices, eyes blank and devoid of life, lips pressed into a constant line, stuck between a frown and a smile. Now, as she looks around, Alora can see just how bright the screen light is on everyone's faces, casting each person's skin in an almost sickly glow.

I never noticed how close we hold them to our faces, Alora thinks to herself as she's practically pushed by the crowd into the tram station. People keep running into each other, shoulder-checking strangers without uttering an apology or even reacting, which makes Alora feel queasy.

"Did I ever do that?" she asks herself, but she can barely recall anything other than the media on her E-Device. For the first time today, she frowns, worrying suddenly about what all she's done while she's been distracted. Some of these people are getting straight-up knocked over, and even as they fall, they don't dare to tear their eyes away from whatever carbon copy video they're watching.

It's quite alarming, and as the tram arrives, gliding to a graceful stop along its tracks, Alora is very relieved people will be sitting down instead of bulldozing into each other. As she settles into an uncomfortable seat, Alora watches the people flood in around her, a massive school of fish going with the flow, no real direction in mind.

She studies their grim faces, their eye colors, their noses, their lips; each person is drastically different from the other. All their clothes match, she realizes, with the same monochrome color palette. Each person is wearing deep misty grays, inky blacks, and accents of bright white. Though some wear shorts, some wear pants, or skirts that don't reach their knees to skirts that drag on the floor. It reminds Alora once more about her bitter discovery yesterday. Everything seems to be a near carbon copy of the next thing and it's spreading to the people. Their E-Devices tell them what to wear after all, or rather, the fabricated AI influencers do. It's not as though she can expect anything else, as frustrating as it is.

Alora looks down at herself, frowning as she realizes she's also wearing the same colors. She hadn't put much thought into her outfit this morning; never having to think about it before, she just blindly grabbed what she usually does and threw it on.

Just as the tram is about to close its doors, a girl, who looks to be no more than two years older than Alora, glides past with a strikingly graceful stride compared to the other people. Alora looks up immediately, drawn to the uniqueness, and finds that this girl seems to be quite different in many ways. The first thing Alora notices is her hair. In a sea of natural colors, this girl's blonde hair is decorated with streaks of pink, blotches of baby blues, and spatters of sugar-sweet purple.

The girl's outfit catches Alora's attention next. It's the first one Alora has seen all day with true colors, and a lot at that. She's wearing a bright sweater, made up of a multi-colored square pattern, each color is pastel and bright, complementing the girl's deep purple skirt, white knee-high socks, and black loafers. Alora blinks a couple of times to keep her eyes from watering, both from the sudden array of colors and the resounding instant bond she feels towards the girl.

As Alora studies her, she never assumed the girl would be studying her right back. She's so distracted by the girl's shining creativity that she never even notices the biggest thing setting her apart from everyone else on the tram is that she also doesn't have an E-Device.

"Hello," the girl acknowledges her from across the aisle, nearly making Alora jump up from her seat.

Alora's gaze quickly shifts back up to meet the mysterious stranger's, who is grinning and beholding warm brown eyes sparkling with mirth. Alora doesn't know what to say; she's never talked to an actual person before, and even as she opens her mouth, trying to greet the kind girl, nothing comes out. Her cheeks heat with embarrassment, and she quickly shuts her mouth, picturing herself looking like a shocked goldfish. The colorful girl just laughs, but the sound isn't unkind.

"I'm Dahlia," the girl introduces herself, "what's your name?"

"Alora," she stammers in response, grateful Dahlia gave her an easy introduction.

"That's a lovely name!" Dahlia's voice is filled with elation. Alora can tell just by looking at her slightly lopsided smile, Dahlia means what she says.

"You don't have an E-Device," Alora observes, kicking herself internally for pointing out what's glaringly obvious.

"Neither do you," Dahlia replies, seeming very happy about the fact.

Alora nods already worryingly lost on what to say. For a brief moment, it's completely silent again, and Alora fidgets with her fingers, feeling the beginnings of awkwardness settling heavily on her shoulders. She doesn't want to ruin her first time talking to an actual person, especially someone so interesting, and who clearly enjoys creating, like herself. So, Alora takes a deep calming breath and breaks the quiet, "I, uhm," she pauses, her heart hammering hard in her chest and her nerves drawn tight, but pushing forward, "I like your hair," Alora finishes.

Dahlia beams right away, her smile widening into a full-on grin, "I did it myself!" she bursts with pride.

There's an undertone Alora doesn't miss, a worry Alora might question Dahlia for even considering doing something that a robot could do for her or judge her for being different. Alora feels the weight of her nerves disappear almost immediately, as she realizes the girl sitting across from her is just like her, nervous and trapped in a world curated to drain creativity and waste talent. "That's so cool!" Alora exclaims, trying her hardest to show Dahlia, she truly means it, even if she's not used to talking.

It doesn't take long for the two girls to become friends; they talk through the entire tram ride. Alora spills her secret about losing her E-Device and how she discovered writing, and Dahlia jokingly welcomes her to a life without electronics. Alora learns Dahlia loves fashion, makes her own clothes, dyes her own hair, and hasn't touched an E-Device for two whole years.

"I have a group of friends who all like to make their own things, without E-Devices. If you want, you can come hang out with us sometime," Dahlia enthusiastically shares.

"I would love to!" Alora is no longer whispering, far too excited to have met someone like her. By the time Alora reaches her stop, she's made her first friend, and hopefully, many more to come.

"Good luck with getting that notebook!" Dahlia says as Alora rises from her seat. "I can't wait to read what you create, Alora!"

"See you soon!" Alora calls back, exiting the tram at a completely new station. She's so happy she's nearly skipping to the meeting spot, humming a tune the whole way there. Everything just keeps getting better and better, especially now that she knows she's not alone!

Getting the notebook is easy; the seller left it in the lobby of the complex, which is the first one directly outside the tram station. Alora supposes she's lucky; if she had to try to find her way to it without a GPS, it could have proven difficult. Then again, Alora's in the mood for adventure now, and anything out of the *ordinary* will help her come up with story ideas. The security bot in the lobby quickly scans Alora's face, making sure she's the right person, and delicately hands her the notebook and pencil packet without a fuss. Alora stares down at them for a moment, feeling the slight weight of the objects in her hand. She holds the future in her grasp, and the thought sends a thrill through her. This, right here, is where her story starts, where her life truly begins, and she can't wait another second for it.

As she heads back home, her mind is flooded with opportunities. *What will she write? Who will she meet?* It is overwhelming. Alora's innovation is ignited. After living in a void for so long, she is finally fulfilling the aching need for achievement in her chest, and ready to chase away the dull drawl of repetition.

8

Friendship

When she got home, Alora was excited to explore and order new clothes, ones with as much color as she could find, even if they still adhered to the dull browns, grays, and blacks of everyone around her. She didn't mind using up the rest of her monthly allowance, for a chance to blend in slightly better with Dahlia and her friends.

Once again, the following day, Alora was dressed and ready in record time, making it to the kitchen and receiving the same programed morning monologue from Ms.E46.

For breakfast today, Alora is blessed with pancakes. She eagerly fills her plate with one of each kind: chocolate, blueberry, strawberry, and the regular plain classic.

"May I have some syrup?" Alora asks Ms.E46, unable to keep newfound cheer out of her voice. The robot gives a jerky nod and passes Alora the maple syrup.

"You have not had maple syrup since you were five years old. Are you experiencing dietary changes?" Ms.E46 questions Alora, no doubt trying to catalog the change and add it to her extensive database, 'how to correctly care for a teenage girl'.

"Yes," Alora replies, deciding it's much easier to just agree than to try to explain to an artificial maid her desire to explore unfamiliar routines. "I will probably be trying a lot of new diets," she adds hoping Ms.E46 will remember and not question her about it later.

A soft whir sounds from Ms.E46, and small puffs of steam pool from the venting slits on the back of her TV-like head as she downloads and stores the new information.

"Excellent," the robot finally concludes, "I am ready to produce any food item your new diet requires of you, child number ten billion seven hundred eighty-two." As anticipated, promptly stated, and, although her fake voice remained as monotone and automated as usual, Alora can almost conjure up an eagerness behind it, making a game of pretending Ms.E46 secretly does have feelings, much like a real person. Now that Alora's sworn herself from using E-Devices as much as possible, the difference in what she can actually think up is striking. Where she once had a passing thought about Ms.E46 actually caring for her beyond her programming, she now visualizes whole scenarios about how Ms.E46 would act if she were human. It'd be like having a mother, Alora realizes, and for once, the thought makes her sad. She never focused her thinking much on her mother, doesn't even remember the woman who gave her life. Alora never considered her upbringing to be *different* because she didn't have her mother. But now, Alora's reconsidering.

Last night, when she arrived home with her notebook and pencils, as treasure in her hands, she had thousands of ideas about what to write, rampaging through her head like a stampede of spooked antelopes. She'd filled nearly five pages with her own, original stories, things her exceptional imagination curated. Thrilled about writing, finally fulfilling the void of boredom gnawing hungrily in her chest, Alora didn't really give much thought to what she was actually penning. Thinking back now, every story she wrote last night had something to do with a lonely girl, one without friends or parents or a pet to play with. Much like herself.

Alora never wanted these things before, nor had the capacity and attention span to contemplate the idea of true friendship, or the need for real interaction plaguing her now. It's what's driving her forward, through the fear of meeting new people and the sickening worry that they won't like her.

Alora needs people, she realizes; friends and humans who she can talk to and create with face-to-face. She's seen it in movies, older ones that came out long before she was born, close tight-knit families with the qualities she now hopes to cultivate. People used to spend special days together, celebrating birthdays and holidays, which Alora has personally never experienced. Not only does she want that, but she also longs for it almost as much as she craved creating with her own two hands, and today, that's what she's going to get.

Today, I'm going to make new friends, Alora thinks to herself as she scarfs down her pancakes, reveling in their sweet taste. Real friends who aren't AI or robots programmed to like her and mimic her interests like mindless clones of herself. Her new life started yesterday and this is just one more step forward in the right direction.

Alora leaves the house a little early, determined to make a good first impression. She's so nervous she can practically taste it. It's a jittery feeling, mixing with her excitement, making her heart do backflips in her chest as she makes her way towards the tram station once more. She can't remember the last time she ever traveled this much in just a few days, much less with an actual purpose. She used to ride the tram every once in a while, just to get out of the house to stretch her legs, but would wind up just sitting and staring at her E-Device for hours on end, going around in a loop from stop to stop, until she got too hungry to cycle around any longer.

Not this time, though, much like when she went to get her notebook, she's moving with a purpose. She pays attention to every number that flies by, every stop that's called out, until she reaches the one Dahlia gave her. Alora had even written the number down in the back of her notebook so she wouldn't forget, stop number 2551. The weather here was colder, and the wind howled angrily. Alora knows the tram can zoom across states and countries with ease in just an hour or two, but she's never paid attention to the true differences of each en-vironment. She shivers, goosebumps rising on her skin. Alora crosses her arms over her middle, trying to warm herself up.

She looks around quickly for Dahlia, who promised she would be waiting when she exited the tram. But this station is much larger than the one by Alora's home, and there are swarms of people on their E-Devices wan-dering aimlessly around her. Alora tries to spot any splotch of color in the crowd, remembering what Dahlia said about creating her own clothes, but it's hard to see through the large mob. She tries to push forward, weaving through the distracted people. Some of them are wearing coats, while others aren't, leading Alora to wonder how they aren't cold. Perhaps they're all too absorbed in their electronics to notice. She passes a woman in a black dress that's cut just above her knees and hugs her body gently. The woman's lips are turning blue, her skin pale and frigid, but she never lets her eyes stray from whatever video she is so enraptured by.

Alora makes it to the entrance of the tram station without seeing even a glimpse of dyed blonde hair or the warm brown eyes of her friend. Panic is already beginning to settle in; her heart jumps into her throat, and her stomach feels like it might bottom out. Suddenly, a large, light purple jacket is strewn carefully across her shoulders, "Sorry, I forgot to tell you it's cold here," Dahlia's familiar voice sounds from behind Alora.

When Alora turns, she finds Dahlia frowning at her with concern clear on her features and a silent plea for forgiveness in her brown eyes. Alora just smiles and quickly fits her arms through the sleeves of the jacket, hugging it close to her cold frame. "It's okay," Alora assures her friend quickly, and watches the light immediately flood back into Dahlia's eyes, "I don't mind the cold."

"Are you sure? You looked like you were turning into a popsicle," Dahlia teases, a smile splitting across her face.

"Okay, maybe I mind the cold a little bit," Alora says sheepishly.

Dahlia laughs, a bright, joyful sound that rings through the echoey station, and Alora can't help but smile.

Dahlia leads Alora to her 'clubhouse', which Alora soon figures out is an unused auditorium in the back of a nursing home. The robots there are much more modernized than Ms.E46; their structures are sleek and fully articulated, and their faces are made to look more animated and human, unlike Ms.E46's TV mug.

Dahlia catches Alora eyeing one of the nurse robots that's currently assisting an incredibly old woman with the TV remote and shoots her a questioning glance.

"We don't have robots like this back at home," Alora explains as the two make their way down the hallway, Dahlia's heeled boots clicking softly against the polished floor. "My dad made me one when I was little. It basically raised me and would be much easier to accept if it looked like an actual person," Alora quickly realizes she probably just overshared and was about to shrug it off and change the subject.

Surprisingly, Dahlia responds, "I understand," with a thoughtful nod.

Those two words alone nearly made Alora shatter into a million pieces right where she was standing. She's never heard those words from someone before, never felt the gentle care in simple *understanding*, in companionship. Alora quickly wipes away the tears that once more threaten to rise, not wanting to come across as *more* weird than she's sure she already is.

"I was raised by AI learning websites and robotic nurses," Dahlia continues, her smile never wavering even as she speaks. "It's a little difficult to have a childhood like people used to when your parents are too busy on their own devices to pay you mind." Dahlia glances at Alora, and the look that passes between them is nothing but the appreciation, of knowing exactly what one another has gone through.

"Thank you," Alora responds with sincerity of heart.

"For what?"

"For this, for being my friend, for knowing," Alora rambles slightly, but she needs to get the words out, to let her new friend know just how much this means to her. Dahlia's smile softens, and she nods lightly.

"Of course, we have to stick together, right? There are only so many of us who aren't always on electronics after all," Alora exclaims, her excitement coming back tenfold as they reach the entrance of the auditorium.

"Ready to meet everyone else?" Dahlia asks softly, her hand poised on the door, ready to push.

Alora feels her nerves coming back, rising to the surface like bubbles in a boiling pot of water. But, looking at Dahlia, at her joy and the way she practically bounces with anticipation, her anxiety eases. Dahlia's by her side, and soon, hopefully, the others will be too.

"I'm ready," Alora takes a deep breath, clearing her mind and reminding herself, *this is day one of my new life, of a better life. I've got this.*

Dahlia opens the door and holds it wide for Alora to enter.

I've been ready for this my whole life, the thought calms her, steadies her, and she walks confidently into the room with Dahlia by her side.

9

Bonding Alora stands frozen in the doorway for just a moment as three pairs of eyes all dart towards her staring yet not judging the way her nerves have been screaming they would. No, Dahlia's three friends seem more curious than anything else. In fact, they seem just as over-joyed as Dahlia was to find another person who was like them, who felt the same way they do. Alora's suspicions are only confirmed when a short girl with cropped brown hair and large bright eyes shoots up from her spot on the carpeted floor and rushes towards Alora and tackles her in a massive hug.

"Hi!" the girl squeals, practically wiggling with excitement, "I'm Kit," finally letting go and backing up enough to look Alora in the eyes.

The girl seems young, at least two years younger than everyone else. Her smile is bright and warm. She rocks back and forth on the heels of her pink shoes. Like Dahlia, her clothes are a multitude of colors, but they're starker than Dahlia's and much more unorganized.

Trying to blink out of her shock at the sudden onslaught of affection from the younger girl, she introduces herself, "Hi, I'm Alora."

"Oh, I know!" Kit holds her head slightly higher as if pleased by her knowledge.

"I maybe, sort of, kind of, told everyone about you," Dahlia confesses, coming to stand beside Alora, giving her a supportive sheepish smile. "I was just so ecstatic to introduce you."

Alora responds with a genuine smile of her own and expresses her gratitude, "Thank you."

Dahlia looks immediately relieved that Alora isn't upset.

Why would she be? It saves her from anxiously introducing herself or awkwardly stumbling over her own name. At least this way, the others already knew what to expect when meeting her.

A boy, around Alora's age, with shaggy black hair and pale skin, gets up from his seat where he was hunched over his own notebook. He takes his pencil, which looks much shorter than Alora's, almost as if it's been cut in half, and tucks it delicately behind his ear.

"Give her some space, Kit!" he hollers, crossing his thin arms over his chest, while a smile tugs at the corner of his lips. He's wearing all black from head to toe. His body is swallowed up by a massive hoodie with the name of an icon rock and roll band etched across the front in bold white letters. He catches Alora's gaze briefly; his eyes are hazel, a blend between sea green and chestnut brown, and there are dark circles under them like he hasn't slept in a while. He lowers his eyes nearly as quickly as he makes eye contact, looking down at his feet.

"I'm Victor," he mumbles, so quietly Alora barely hears him, "and that's my sister, Lula." He nods towards the last girl in the room, who gives Alora a polite smile. She's older, maybe even older than Dahlia. She doesn't look like

Victor; her skin is tanned like she's spent days on end out in the sun, and her eyes are blue. Her hair is the same, though, long, straight, and black, cutting off just above her waist. Her clothes are covered in splotches of color, but it's not a part of the fabric like Kit and Dahlia's clothes. It's more like someone flung the color on top of her and let it dry there, kind of like a stain.

"It's nice to meet you, Alora," Lula says, her voice gentle and kind.

"It's nice to meet you, too," Alora emphasizes, "all of you, I mean," she adds, feeling the heated flush of embarrassment crawl up her neck. The feeling is easily overshadowed by the welcoming atmosphere and the kindness of the others in the room.

Dahlia reaches for Alora's hand, her skin warm, the weight of her fingers intertwined with Alora's brings an unnamable comfort. Dahlia pulls Alora deeper into the room, bringing her to the long rectangular table in the center. She pulls out a chair for her friend, grinning the whole time, and sits down next to her. Alora sets her own notebook and pencils down on the table, receiving a quiet whistle of awe from Victor, who sits down across from the two.

"You got fresh pencils?" he asks eagerly, eyes fixated solely on the wooden objects in their cardboard package.

"I think so," Alora says, feeling a little shy because she doesn't really know what new pencils actually look like. For all she knows, these could be nearly used up.

Victor takes his eyes off the package for a moment to look at her and nods, a small smile shaping his face. He grabs the pencil he tucked behind his ear and slides it in the space between them.

"They get duller the more you use them," he keeps explaining, "when they get dull enough, they don't write anymore, and you have to sharpen them by cutting off the sides until the gray part is sharp again."

Alora nods, her eyes fixed on the pencil between them instead of on him. She's worried if she looks at him while he's talking, he'll get shy again. She heard from Ms.E46 once that keeping eye contact during a conversation is polite, but she doesn't want to ruin her chances to make a new friend, or to learn!

"You must write a lot," Alora remarks, noting how stubby his pencil looks compared to hers.

"Yeah, I write poems," Victor's voice is full of pride as he speaks, "I can show you. I mean, if you'd like?"

Alora can swear he puffed his chest a little, like a lion satisfied with its hunt. Alora suppresses a smile at the thought; she doesn't want him to think she's laughing at him. In fact, she thinks it's admirable to be so open and so ready to share your work. It would definitely take a lot of courage for her to show anyone the snippets of stories she's been writing, espe-cially when everyone else seems so talented and much more experienced.

Alora spends the rest of her day reading through Victor's notebook. His poems are good, spectacular even. In truth, they started out dry and a little dull, much like her stories right now. They describe the tram rides and the view outside the window. They actually seem to follow the same order of events and feelings Alora experienced when she first felt boredom. He has a poem about the sunlight, the way it feels, and it takes her back to when she rushed outside and how the sun felt on her skin as it set. His writing developed better and better from there, deeper, more meaningful, harder to understand, but in a way making her brain tickle instead of spiking frustration.

Each line beholding so much emotion, fueled with imagery, making Alora feel as if she's inside his writing, personally partaking in every word and in tune with each detail. It's magical, like she can travel between worlds or see into Victor's life and into his experiences.

He moves his hands in the direction of his notebook but instead fidgets with his jacket sleeve. He never stops her from reading. Occasionally, he frowns when Alora gets to a piece he doesn't like as much, mumbling excuses like, "I had writers block that day," or, "I couldn't find the right rhyme to fit there."

Victor was his own toughest critic. His words are absolutely captivating Alora. Thankfully, he never stops her from exploring, and he smiles at every praise that leaves her lips.

"Your writing is amazing!" Alora proclaims when she reaches the end of his poems. There was a lot to read through, but it was so engaging, she didn't even notice the time passing.

Now that Alora has returned from her poetic adventure, she looks around and realizes, Dahlia left her seat by Alora's side and was excitedly talking to Kit about new clothes and Lula paused her project to have a small snack on the carpet next to them.

"Nah, it's nothing special," Victor says, but she can tell by the sound of his voice he's pleased with himself.

"How do you write so neatly?" Alora asks, staring down at the letters on the page. She recalls the words in her notebook; they look like intelligible scribbles next to Victor's neat handwriting.

Victor lights up like a lamp, "I can show you!" enthusiastically reaching out and plucking his notebook from Alora's hands. He flips to a new blank page and grips his stubby pencil preparing to write. The way he positions it is different than holding a fork or a spoon, like Alora's been doing. He writes a few words across the page.

"You have to hold it like this," he demonstrates as he writes, angling his hand so Alora has a good view of the way he's gripping it.

Alora nods, peering closer to get a better look, "That looks uncomfortable," she says skeptically, but Victor just laughs.

"Yeah, it was at first," he confirms, "but it gets easier and you'll write way quicker this way, wanna try?" He hands her the pencil and pushes his notebook across the table towards her with an almost hopeful look in his eyes.

Alora tries to copy Victor's technique. She looks up at Victor for confirmation and he nods in encouragement. He's wearing a large smile now and all his earlier shyness has evaporated. He reaches out and gently corrects her hold.

Alora's fingers immediately start to cramp. She can feel the ache forming in her muscles, but Victor verifies she is doing it correctly. Alora frowns slightly, but moves the pencil towards the paper anyway, and writes all the letters of the alphabet. To her delight, each one is clear and precise, almost as if she were typing!

"Keep practicing and it'll feel more natural," Victor assures her, transfixed on her letters, "I promise."

Alora nods, handing Victor his pencil back with a quiet thank you.

Alora spends the rest of the quickly passing day with her new friends. Lula is an artist and shows off her paintings, come to find out, which is also why her clothes are spattered in color. Alora gawks at the images; they're like pictures coming out of Lula's mind, projected perfectly onto a canvas. Lula explains she paints what she sees outside and adds things afterwards. Alora's favorite piece is a field of wildflowers, which don't grow anymore because of all the fake plastic grass. In the center of the painted field, Kit and Dahlia are laughing and playing around in flowy dresses flaunting intricate floral patterns.

Kit was eager to sing for Alora, putting on her own little concert. Everyone indulged by clapping and singing along, even without any background music. Kit creates her own lyrics and sheet music, even though no one here plays an instrument. Alora learns about Kit's hope, one day, to be able to learn how to play; she just needs to find an instrument that actually works.

As the end of their time together draws to a close, Alora feels like she's part of a family. There's something about *this* group, each of them sharing their talents with her, working so hard on their own projects, that inspires her. It pushes her even harder to write her own stories, to *not* only create but to highlight what she's made, showcasing what's special about her.

It's dark now, the sun almost fully set outside the nursing home windows. One of the nurse robots enters, warning them visitor time is over and it's time for them to leave. Alora helps Lula pack up her paintings, making sure she's as careful as possible as she slides them gently into the cupboard.

Dahlia has to walk Kit home, so Alora heads to the train station with Victor and Lula. Victor leads the way, too far ahead to hear Alora and Lula's conversation.

"So, Dahlia told us you like to write," Lula says, as they make their way back to the tram station.

Alora hugs her journal and pencils closer to her chest and nods, "Yeah, I want to write stories."

"Want to?" Lula asks gently, glancing over to her.

"I don't think I'm too good at it," Alora explains, looking down at her feet.

There's a pause, but the silence isn't heavy; it's softer, thoughtful, and Alora can practically hear the gears turning in Lula's head.

"Practice is the only way to get better. Practice makes perfect," Lula finally responds, her voice coaxing. "You like writing, right?"

"I *love* it," Alora confirms.

"Then it doesn't matter if you're good at it; what matters is you're having fun."

Alora thinks about Lula's words the whole tram ride home, while trying her best to also listen to what Victor is saying. The siblings exit a few stops before her own, and she's left alone in the tram, staring down at the notebook across her lap. She practices holding her pencil, pressing it to the paper, then putting it away. Her few pages of scribbles don't seem nearly as grand as they were to her before.

Practice makes perfect, Lula's voice cuts through the doubt in Alora's head, making her smile slightly. The older girl is right. She didn't start this to show off to anyone else; she started this because she needed to create. Alora needs to write, just like Lula needs to paint and Kit needs to sing.

When Alora gets to her stop, she rushes home. Tonight, she's starting an actual story. Tonight, she's making characters, a plot, and everything else a story needs. She's got friends by her side to teach her and support her.

Nothing's going to hold her back ever again. It's just like she thought before she entered that room: she's ready for this, she's been born ready for this. The next time she meets up with her friends in the old auditorium, she's going to have an entire chapter of a story ready for them to read, and it's going to be good.

Motivation

Since her first day with the 'Creators', the group name Kit gave their quintet, Alora's never looked back. *Why would she?* She's so much happier now! Without using electronics, she does such a variety of fulfilling things.

In fact, Alora's been getting up when the sun rises each morning just because she wants to. Today is no different. Alora stares out of her bedroom window, propped up on the corner of her bed, with a real and true smile brightening her face. She's still trying to rub the sleep from her eyes, but the view is worth rising early. After an entire life of trying to shut the curtains as far as possible, to barricade herself from the outside world to overindulge in her own personal digital fairyland, Alora doesn't want to miss a single second of everything she's unknowingly neglected.

She's long since torn down the blackout curtains, which lay neatly folded in a bare corner of her room; a room that is brighter now, and not just because of the sunlight. The space is decorated with paintings from Lula, crocheted blankets from Dahlia, a mixture of Victor's poetry, and some of her favorite sheet music from Kit strewn up on the wall. She still can't fully understand the musical scales herself, but Kit's been helping her learn as a past time.

Alora's closet is filled with familiar clothes that are now spattered in paint from helping Lula, or droplets of ink from Victor, who has been trying to learn to use an ink pen, or simply bleached and dyed by Dahlia. There are some new editions in there too; friendship bracelets Kit keeps making, crocheted stuffed animals Dahlia's been obsessed with recently, and a stack of notebooks Alora plans to fill front to back when she finishes the one she has.

Her current notebook sits softly in her lap as she looks out at the streaks of pink and the gentle oranges lighting up the morning sky.

She wiggles her pencil in between her fingers, the rubbery pink end, which she's learned from Victor, is called an eraser, and taps against her notebook cover with each movement.

Alora uses each sunrise as motivation for her newest short story about a young girl who lives in a castle on a cloud and watches the world go by around her. Alora showed it off once or twice to her friends, who've been incredibly supportive. It's the first story she's actually been proud of, one that feels real and not forced. Sometimes the words flow from her mind and onto the page like the pencil is guiding her instead of the other way around. She nearly feels like an actual writer now, not only because the others like it, they would support her no matter how bad it was, but because when she reads what she's written, she can feel her own story. It's not quite a masterpiece yet, but she loves it, and that's what matters. Alora is improving, just as Lula had said on their first tram ride back home nearly half a year ago.

Thinking of the tram ride, reminds Alora she must start getting ready if she doesn't want to be late to the weekly Creator meet-up! She takes her time, delicately placing her beloved notebook and pencil on her desk, which is littered with pieces of paper she's ripped from her notebook. She smiles as she looks at the papers.

She originally started ripping out pages when she was frustrated with her writing. Times when the content on the page didn't make sense or didn't come out the way she wanted it to, she balled them up in her hand and threw them to the floor, as if the writing was nothing but trash. But, in the face of the slop AI reuses over and over, even Alora's *trash* as a very new writer is considered gold. So, she collected all the balled-up garbage, put it on her desk, and rewrote until the old became new and beautiful. Turning from something she was ashamed of into something she had fixed up, a wounded bird beginning to fly again. It's routine now, whenever something doesn't come out well, to place the page here, clear her mind, and come back to it until she can write it the way she sees it in her head.

Alora moves to the bathroom, getting ready for the day, and picks out a comfortable outfit. She shrugs on the lavender jacket Dahlia made for her and slips her feet into colorful shoes. They used to be completely black, but Kit had somehow gotten her hands on a packet of sparkly crystal-like beads, and the whole quintet of Creators spent their entire day pushing the beads onto their shoelaces until each and every one of their shoes sparkled.

Alora heads down the hall to get her breakfast from Ms.E46, who attributes Alora's recent happiness to the 'new diet' the robot is serving. Light pours into the hall from the kitchen; all the overhead artificial lights have been shut off for a while now, letting the sun light up her home. It's fresher, warmer, much more comforting than the harsh fluorescents used to be, and on mornings as exciting as this, Alora can't ask for anything more.

Today isn't just another day of meeting her friends, she's always excited for that. On this specific day, Alora is going to propose for the Creators to try something new. Well, not entirely new, but something she really deeply hopes they'll want to try out as much as she does.

She slides into her seat around the dining room table, saying an unconscious "thank you" to Ms.E46, as the robot hands her a fresh warm plate of eggs, ham, and toast. When she's done eating, she brings her dishes to the sink herself, instead of making Ms.E46 do it for her and begins to clean. The first time she did this, Ms.E46 almost short-circuited, her programming struggling to adapt to the idea that a person could do her job. She wasn't trying to make the robot glitch; she just wanted to learn how to do it for herself. So, although she leaves all the other dishes unwashed, her own plate and utensils sit fresh and clean in the otherwise empty drying rack.

The tram ride to the Creators' meeting location is quiet, as always, but it gives Alora enough time to rethink all her possible proposals to pitch her new idea. Her hand unconsciously drifts down to the knitted bag slung over her shoulder, where her notebook and pencil packet lie safe and secure. She wants to make it sound as enticing as possible, because it could mean a lot of work. Then again, creating and doing what they all love is never really work, it just takes a little motivation.

Lula and Victor join her halfway through the ride. She wasn't able to save seats for them this time. It's hard to reserve spots when other passengers aren't paying attention to anything but the device in their hands. So, the two sat a cart down from her. She can see them through the window in the divider at least, and Victor waves at her, mouthing a cheerful 'good morning'. Lula gives her usual smile and a small nod of her head. Alora waves in return, before settling back into her seat. With her friends so close, she relaxes slightly more, although the tram seat is too uncomfortable for her to enjoy the ride fully.

It doesn't take much longer to get to tram station 2251. Alora bounces to her feet and rushes out the doors, meeting Victor and Lula at the entrance of the station. The three make their way to the nursing home together. The walk isn't bad, now that the snow has gone away, and it isn't so chilly out.

As anticipated, face to face real life conversations! Lula talks about her latest painting, while Victor impatiently waits for his turn to show Alora his newest poems. It feels as if it only took a few minutes to get to the nursing home when it's probably taken far longer. Time works funny that way, whenever Alora is with her friends, the world zips by in a flash, but she never feels like she's missed any of it. She can't think of anything more important than her group, her friends, nothing else can truly compare.

Alora greets some of the residents of the home as she makes her way to the auditorium, long past needing someone to remind her which turns to take or what doors to go through. Kit and Dahlia are already waiting for the three inside. Kit springs forward, hugging Alora so tightly she almost bursts, before moving to Victor, who tries, and fails, to worm his way out of Kit's embrace.

"Hey, Alora, got any more of that story?" Dahlia asks, pulling Alora away from the chaos of Kit and Victor for a moment. Lula already slipped away, back to her paintings, trying to avoid the storm of affection that is their youngest friend.

"Actually, I do!" Alora fishes her notebook out of her bag and hands it over to Dahlia, who grins brightly and beelines towards the table so she can read the newest addition.

Kit, realizing Lula's escaped her enthusiasm, frees Victor and rushes over to Lula instead, like a puppy laying eyes on their favorite person.

Victor glances over towards Alora with a look she can only describe as baffled, and Alora can't help but break out into laughter. He grins too, rolling his eyes at her, "It's not funny! I'm going to have bruises!" he says in mock annoyance.

Eventually, everyone settles down. Kit is helping Lula paint, Victor is reading Alora's newest chapter after Dahlia finished it, and Dahlia is crocheting another stuffed animal out of some new super soft material she managed to get for cheap. Alora nervously clears her throat. The sound is loud in the comfortable silence, but the homey atmosphere never breaks, it doesn't even waver.

"Guys," Alora says hesitantly, earning the eyes of everyone in the room, "I have an idea I want to suggest."

"I love ideas!" Kit interjects with a bright smile, her eyes encouraging. She leans on the edge of her seat as if the next words Alora speaks will change her life.

"I was just wondering if...," she pauses, swallowing hard. She's never been shy around her friends but somehow asking them this makes her feel uncomfortable. She pushes forward anyway, taking a deep breath and squaring her shoulders, ready for them to completely shut her down, "if... you would want to make something together, like a play or something, combining all our talents?" Alora squeezes her eyes shut, bracing herself, as though their disapproval will be a physical blow.

"I want to do a play!" Kit pipes up immediately, shooting to her feet like the idea heaved her into its arms and pulled her up. "I heard there were plays with a lot of music and people used to love to sing their songs all the time!" Her voice is bright and loud, flooded to the brim, with unbridled excitement.

"A play could be a nice challenge," Lula offers, "I'd love to paint the backdrops."

"I'll help Kit with songs!" Victor adds quickly, "There's a lot of depth in musicals, right? You'll need a poet for that."

"I'll make costumes!" Dahlia exclaims, looking to Alora with shining eyes, "That is, of course, if you'll do us the honor of giving us characters."

Alora is nearly taken aback by their eagerness, her friends' readiness to do this with her, to trust her with such a project, and to build a play around her vision and writing. It's nearly enough to make her cry. A smile splits across her face, she can never seem to stop smiling around them, and she nods so enthusiastically she almost gives herself whiplash.

"Alright," she concludes, "let's do this!"

Just like that, Alora's ideas, birthed in her imagination, are once more set into motion. Aided by her friends, who're all buzzing with their input, the thought of developing something altogether empowers them to dream even further. By the end of the day, Alora already knows what she wants their play to be about. As she makes her trip back home, to her desk where she can't wait to put all the bullet points in her head into motion, she's reminded once again that she isn't alone anymore. They've got this together.

Creation It took Alora nearly an entire month to write out the play to the best of her ability. The process was long. She wrote from sunrise to sunset and couldn't have enjoyed it more. For once in her life, she had a purpose, a need to create for herself and for her friends. She wrote the play, then rewrote it, then rewrote it again, until it came out exactly as she wanted. When she showed the final draft to the other Creators, they were overjoyed. They loved their characters, and the story, and were eager to get to work. It only took them a couple of weeks to put together the rest.

Now, in their auditorium, a makeshift stage, made from cardboard shipping boxes that Dahlia had stored up at home, sits in the corner. It's not too big, it can't hold more than two people at once, but it's good enough for the set of a play. Especially with the different backgrounds, painted by Lula, that can easily be swapped out from scene to scene. Her workmanship on each board is absolutely breathtaking, as if she plucked the scenes straight from Alora's inventiveness and painted them onto the canvas until they were mastered to perfection.

Dahlia took down the old, framed AI-generated pictures from the wall, so she could hang the costumes from the nails. Each outfit is heavily detailed, each strip of fabric serving a purpose, each color blending beautifully with the others. Alora can tell Dahlia spared no expense when making them, and she can't be more grateful to her best friend for going all out.

Victor and Kit took a while to make the music, each lyric and rhyme carefully planned and reviewed, for weeks on end. Victor helped Kit with some of the harder rhymes, utilizing the deeper emotions he usually pours into his poetry. Kit wrote everything down and incorporated her musical knowledge to decide the notes and pitch. Each and every song they created was authentic and purposeful. The two of them went through an entire journal making sure it was perfect.

Which brings the Creators to today, walking through the doors of the auditorium together, into a room prepped for a play they've poured their hearts and souls into. Alora clutches her notebook to her chest as she looks around the room, ecstatically analyzing how each piece came together. The stage, the backgrounds, the script, the costumes, and the songs, all of it is physical, concrete evidence of every minute of creativity, and the time they spent imagining and dreaming. Finally, the proof Alora and her friends can design and build anything they put their minds to without needing help from electronics, is abundantly clear.

The group stands in awe for a moment as everything suddenly becomes real. They've made an entire play, just like people used to do in the past, with nothing but their bare hands and their own minds. No screens, no E-Devices, just people, working together, thinking collectively, and striving to invent some-thing all their own. Alora can't help the tears welling up in her eyes. It feels like a miniature sun is rising in her chest bright and warm and yellow with joy. She looks beside her to see Dahlia, her best friend, with a large grin on her face and the same marveling look in her eyes.

Victor is the first to break the mind-blown silence, "Holy cow, we actually did it." He breathes in disbelief from where he stands on the other side of Alora. He sniffles softly, bringing the sleeve of his hoodie up to his eyes to wipe away his own salty tears. When he catches the others staring, he shoves his hands into his pockets and quickly clears his throat. His eyes drop to the floor, and he rocks on his heels subconsciously.

"I mean, of course we did it! I just can't articulate how much better it is than I envisioned!" he tries to explain, his face becoming redder with each word as it leaves his mouth.

"It's amazing!" Kit practically squeals, saving Victor from his mortification. As if pulled forward by an unseen force, Kit advances deeper into the room, eyes wide with excitement like she is seeing it for the first time again. The look on her face is pure joy, her eyes are lit up and shining like a thousand stars, and her smile stretches so wide it's hurting her face. Lula laughs lightly as she watches Kit spin in a circle, drinking it all in at once.

"I think we all did an amazing job," Lula agrees before glancing over at Alora. "Thank you, for suggesting this. It was good painting practice."

"Thank you for helping make my idea come true," Alora's voice is a pool of gratitude, her heart suddenly feeling three times bigger, surrounded by the joy of her friends and the satisfaction of their completed project.

"We're not done yet!" Dahlia reminds them, pulling the attention of the rest of the group. "We still have to perform it," she says giddily.

Kit freezes where she is, Dahlia's words stopping her in her tracks. Suddenly, her eyebrows knit together, her lower lip jutting out in a pout as she turns to face them all again.

"What's wrong, Kit?" Alora asks.

"I just remembered that..." she pauses, her gaze dropping to the floor, looking suddenly incredibly guilty, "well, I know we made this play and all, and it's amazing! But, we'll be the only ones who'll ever see it," she mumbles. Kit's shoulders slump, like some invisible burden is weighing them down.

Alora frowns as she thinks about what Kit just said. They made this whole grand play, it's delightful, and everything all five of them wanted, but what's the point in making something if no one else but you will enjoy it?

"That is true," Victor pipes up again, looking way less thrilled than he had before. "We worked so hard, but we're the only ones who'll ever know it exists." He sighs, the type of heavy sigh that uses his entire chest and comes out in one big, defeated puff of air.

Alora, however, doesn't even bat an eye. Yes, Victor and Kit's words are true, their talents may never be recognized by others or acknowledged outside of this room. It's difficult to think about. In a world so full of electronics and distractions, wondrously jubilating productions like this one are considered *simple and* hidden from public view. Alora knows they didn't do this to impress others, nevertheless, it would be nice to have an audience to share such a purposeful performance with. They created this play, their own individual artwork, and other customized thought filled contributions, for one reason only, and that's to feel the truth of what it means to be human.

To create, to build something all your own, is the foundation of each person's uniqueness. To be able to construct and fill the framework of individuality, to foster innovative ideas, and discover answers to personal curiosities, is such an inherent, profound, and beautiful ability only *people* possess. And, yes, many people have forgotten they have this opportunity and may never remember. Desire for exploits must be reignited to propel people to pursue their dreams. Not for anyone else, but for themselves, just like this play.

"We didn't do this to share it with others," Alora says, her voice gentle, her words flowing from her lips as smoothly as syrup. She doesn't have to think about what she's going to say, because for once it's crystal clear. "We made this for ourselves, to prove we can do so much more than sit and rot on electronics." Alora's voice getting steadier with each word she speaks, "This is our imagination come to life, we put this here with our bare hands." She might be taking her words too far, repeating herself too much, but she can't stop them from coming out. "Even though others may not enjoy it and may never get the chance to feel what we felt when we created this, we'll know. I think that's enough, for me, at least," Alora holds her head high as she finishes her words remembering what Lula told her a while ago, *Create for yourself, do this for you and no one else!* Alora refuels, "No one is in charge of what you can make when you put your mind to use. No one can dictate your imagination, and no one can take it away from you, not AI, not electronics, not a soul or a creature, or anything else. Your creativity, your innovation, it belongs to you. Always."

"Alora's right, we never did this seeking the attention of others," Lula adds.

Kit brightens, nodding slightly. "You guys are right," she murmurs.

Victor doesn't say anything, but his smile is back, and Alora can see a look of determination in his eyes.

Once Dahlia confirms everyone is ready, she hands out their costumes, and they take turns changing in the bathroom. The outfits look even better on, and they fit perfectly.

"These are amazing, Dahlia," Lula exclaims. Dahlia waves her off, saying they're nothing special, but Alora can tell she's flattered.

Victor moves to set up a camera in front of the stage, so all of them can rewatch their own performances whenever they want. The play runs smoothly after that, and each one of them performs their scenes with accuracy and expression.

The opening scene begins with a princess, Dahlia, being captured by a great beast, who is graciously played by Kit. The princess's best friend, Lula, and knight, Victor, race to save her before it's too late! The deeper into the play they get, the more energized the group becomes, as they bring their work to life. After the ending scene, where Lula realizes the great beast was actually bringing Dahlia to safety when it sensed Dahlia's knight was deceptively planning to overthrow her, they're all so electrified they nearly forget their lines, and none of them can stop grinning.

Later, watching their recorded production, all huddled together on the floor on top of old blankets and half-flattened pillows they'd brought from their houses, it felt nearly magical. It seemed better than anything they'd ever seen, surpassing all the movies, the media skits, and the AI videos combined. Maybe it's because it's their own work, but Alora believes it's because, for once, it was something real. Something entirely human-made, and she couldn't have dreamed of anything better.

Epilogue

The tram zips through the underground tunnels quicker than a blink of an eye. Inside the tram, most of the passengers are quiet, their eyes glued to their devices and their faces expressionless. But, in the sea of people who all dress the same, who act the same, who treat the world with the same cold unknowingly emotionlessness, two girls sit. They whisper quietly to one another. One of them holds a strange book in her lap with rings like a binder and a cover made of lavender plastic. The other girl has hair dyed with every color under the sun, and wears clothes with more excitement than most of the tram passengers will ever see in their entire lives.

Their conversation isn't loud, but, for some reason, it's enough to draw the attention of just one, very young girl. She looks to be about seven, though she could be younger. She holds a small, cheaper E-Device in her hand, but the screen lays dark and empty because she forgot to charge it before leaving home, even after all ten warnings. She's always found it hard to respond to the alerts coming only a few minutes apart. To her, minutes feel like hours.

Absently looking at the powered down E-Device stirs up a strange feeling within her. It's almost like disappointment, like when she sees an ad on a website, she swears her parents pay a premium for. Difficult to process, yet, that feeling isn't quite the right fit. The feeling she has now settles in her chest uncomfortably, like a need for something she can't see, an itch to do something, but she can't gauge exactly what.

Looking around the tram, seeking distraction, she becomes an intrigued silent observer of the two girls' conversation. The young girl was instantly fascinated, absorbed in what they were saying. Something about going to meet their friends, other people, *real* people! The ache in her chest grew stronger at the thought.

Their discussion was centered around a 'new project,' the two older girls whispering happily about creating something the young girl couldn't understand. But she was enticed by the word *create*. She generates things all the time with her AI. Yet something within her told her that these two girls weren't talking about AI.

The little girl wonders to herself, *Creation, without electronics? The idea is absurd. It couldn't be possible, right?*

As the tram comes to a stop, and the mechanical overhead voice reads out the number of the stop, the two girls get up to leave. She almost wants to reach out and stop them, to ask them what they meant. She's never had a question before, never thought as much as she is thinking now.

She catches the eye of the girl with the strange book, holding her stare for just a moment. She sees something familiar in the eyes of the stranger, who smiles softly at her. *Could the stranger tell something was wrong?*

Does the feeling the young girl got right after her E-Device shut down surely mean she's unwell?

Without a word, the older girl places her odd book down on the chair she left, and walks away, following her friend. The door closes behind them, but the young girl watches. Even as the tram speeds away, she doesn't tear her eyes away from where the two girls had been sitting. No one moved to take the two empty spots, no one probably noticed.

For a long time, she stares at the odd plastic book the girl left behind. When the little girl reaches her stop, no more than three minutes later, she springs up from her seat faster than she's ever moved before and snatches the book into her arms, cradling it to her chest.

As she leaves the tram, her E-Device lays forgotten in her seat. But she doesn't even notice, in fact, she forgets it the moment she opens the plastic book.

Her eyes land on words, real words, ones that aren't typed. As she reads, a smile begins to form on her face, and the gnawing feeling eating her from the inside out on the tram disappears. She doesn't understand why, but suddenly she feels lighter, a feather in the wind, as if she's found something she's always been meant to see.

Something inside tells her that, as she reads the opening chapter of this odd book, the first real part of her life has just started.

Author's Note

I wrote this book as a part of my senior project, starting in 2025. Although it has always been a dream of mine to write a novel, and bring my imagination to life, this book represents much more than that. I've written this story to remind people that electronics aren't everything. People survived a long time without them. This is not to say all technology is bad, but simply encouragement to pursue the *much more* of life, surpassing entertainment on a screen.

I implore everyone who reads this to consider donating to charities fostering real human creativity. Everything we have built over hundreds of thousands of years has come from someone's imagination. If not for people who had no distractions, the society we have now would be vastly different. Innovation is like a muscle; our creativity can grow weak if we do not use it. If you have the power to donate, please give it consideration.

The next generations are our future; they are the ones who will shape the earth even when we are long gone. Personally, I would love to see a world where the ability to create is celebrated just as much as getting a new phone and is as normalized in the future as wasting hours on social media is in the present.

Thank you for reading, and I hope you always remember, the future is up to you, and your life is what you make it.

About the Author

Melina Trine was born on the Space Coast of Florida and has remained a lifelong resident. Her early childhood years were spent amid the Florida fauna, between the famous Cocoa Beach and the biodiverse Indian River Lagoon estuary, both basked in the inspiring glow of the Space Shuttle program and the burgeoning private rocket space race.

This backdrop fueled her natural affinity to keep her feet amongst all creatures great and small, and her eyes on the horizon, dreaming of stories and adventures where the little things in life can outshine and provide a haven amongst a growingly loud and technologically driven world. Combining her powerful imagination with her natural passion for research and organization, Melina compiled stacks of composition notebooks full of planned-out chapters, character details, and story arcs juxtaposed to dinosaurs and toy ponies.

The COVID-19 virus ended her final year of elementary school early. Always a writer, this unexpected change allowed her the freedom to explore her writing more fully. Fueled further by her creative writing classes and the mentorships she has enjoyed and benefited from, many of her stories are now blooming into their full splendor. While Pencil & Paper is not the first book she has written, it is her first to be published and represents well her writing style and the topics with which she finds purpose. Melina hopes to inspire others to read, to create, and to find purpose in their passions and expression. She hopes her writing helps in some way to fan the flame of her peers and future authors, and she remains grateful to those who have helped and continue to inspire and support her journey.

Please contact Melina Trine to share how this book has impacted you or to place a bulk order for your class, organization, or family & friends.

Email: trine.melina@gmail.com